A HOME for BIRD

Philip C. Stead

A NEAL PORTER BOOK
ROARING BROOK PRESS
NEW YORK

To the homes I have loved
(and those I have not)

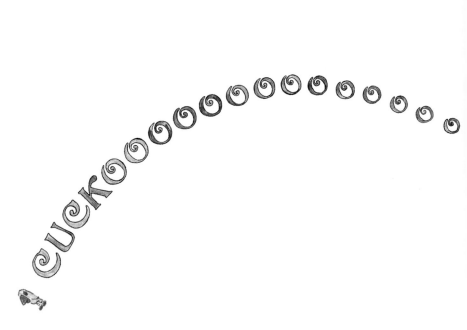

Copyright © 2012 by Philip C. Stead

A Neal Porter Book

Published by Roaring Brook Press

Roaring Brook Press is a division of Holtzbrinck Publishing Holdings Limited Partnership

175 Fifth Avenue, New York, New York 10010

mackids.com

Library of Congress Cataloging-in-Publication Data

Stead, Philip Christian.

   A·home for bird / Philip C. Stead. — 1st ed.

      p. cm.

   "A Neal Porter Book."

   Summary: Vernon the toad takes the silent Bird on a journey in hopes
of finding Bird's home.

   ISBN 978-1-59643-711-1

   [1. Birds—Fiction. 2. Toads—Fiction. 3. Home—Fiction. 4.
Cuckoos—Fiction. 5. Clocks and watches—Fiction.] I. Title.

   PZ7.S808566Hom 2012

   [E]—dc22

                              2011012742

Roaring Brook Press books are available for special promotions and premiums.

For details contact: Director of Special Markets, Holtzbrinck Publishers.

First edition 2012

Printed in China by South China Printing Co. Ltd., Dongguan City, Guangdong Province

10   9   8   7   6   5

V ERNON WAS OUT FORAGING for interesting things
when he found Bird.

"Are you okay?" asked Vernon.
 Bird said nothing.
"Are you lost?"
 Bird said nothing.
"You are welcome to join me," said Vernon.

Vernon introduced Bird to his friends.

"Bird," said Vernon, "meet Skunk and Porcupine."

Bird said nothing.

"Bird is shy," said Vernon, "but also a very good listener."

Vernon showed Bird the river . . .

and the forest.

He took Bird foraging . . .

and cloud watching too.

But Bird said nothing.

"I am worried that Bird is not happy," said Vernon.
"Perhaps he is lost," said Skunk.
"Maybe he misses home," said Porcupine.

So Vernon prepared for a journey to help
Bird find his home.

He readied a boat,

found an oar,

said goodbye to old friends,

and together with Bird, followed the river
into the great unknown.

Vernon showed Bird many different places to live.

"Is this your home?" he asked Bird.

"How about here?"

"Here?"

Vernon sighed. "Bird will speak up when we
find the right home."

But no matter how many places they tried,
Bird said nothing.

And Vernon was sad.

But Vernon was a determined friend.

And with a little help . . .

he and Bird followed the wind.

"I hope this is a good idea," said Vernon.
  Bird said nothing.
"Bird is very brave," thought Vernon.

Having traveled a long way, the two friends came to rest.
"Hello," said Vernon to a kind stranger. "I think we are lost."

The stranger pointed the way . . .

to a house a little farther down the road.

"I am so, so tired," said Vernon.

Bird said nothing.

"Bird is tired too," thought Vernon. "Maybe we'll stop for the night."

Together Vernon and Bird
slid down the curtain,

introduced themselves
to new friends,

and climbed up, up, up to the little house on the wall.

"This home is in need of repair," thought Vernon, carefully placing the door back on its hinges. "I hope Bird doesn't mind."

He put Bird to bed upstairs,

put himself to bed downstairs,

and fell asleep to a gentle sound—
tick-tock, tick-tock, tick-tock . . .

Vernon awoke with the morning light. He liked
this house and the cheerful sounds it made.
"I wonder if Bird likes it too?" thought Vernon.

And Bird said . . .

And Vernon was happy.